Hot Pursuit

Give me
liberty
or give me
death!

—Patrick Henry

Hot Pursuit

Murder in Mississippi

Stacia Deutsch and Rhody Cohon

illustrations by Craig Orback

KAR-BEN
PUBLISHING

Kar-Ben Publishing
A division of Lerner Publishing Group, Inc.
241 First Avenue North
Minneapolis, MN 55401 U.S.A.

Website address: www.karben.com

Library of Congress Cataloging-in-Publication Data

Deutsch, Stacia.
   Hot pursuit / by Stacia Deutsch and Rhody Cohon ; illustrated by Craig Orback.
      p. cm.
    ISBN: 978-0-7613-3955-7 (lib. bdg. : alk. paper)
    1. Schwerner, Michael Henry, 1939-1964—Juvenile literature. 2. Goodman, Andrew, 1943-1964—Juvenile literature. 3. Chaney, James Earl, 1943-1964—Juvenile literature. 4. Mississippi Freedom Project—Juvenile literature. 5. Civil rights workers—Mississippi—Biography—Juvenile literature. 6. African Americans—Civil rights—Mississippi—History—20th century—Juvenile literature. 7. Mississippi—Race relations—History—20th century—Juvenile literature. 8. Neshoba County (Miss.)—Race relations—History—20th century—Juvenile literature. 9. Jewish youth—United States—Biography—Juvenile literature. 10. Jews—United States—Biography—Juvenile literature. I. Cohon, Rhody. II. Orback, Craig, ill. III. Title.
    E185.93.M6D48 2010
    323.092—dc22   2008033479

Manufactured in the United States of America
1 – VI – 12/15/09

Justice denied anywhere diminishes justice everywhere.

—Martin Luther King Jr.

Michael Schwerner could hear the police siren getting nearer and knew he had a decision to make, a decision that might determine if he and his friends lived or died.

"Mickey, what should I do? Should I stop the car or gun the engine and make a run for it?" J.E. Chaney asked, gripping the steering wheel so hard the veins on his hands were bulging. "The police 'round here bring nothing but trouble."

"I agree," Andrew Goodman chimed in. "But it might be worse if we don't stop." Andrew turned his head to look out the back window.

Mickey peered into the side view mirror. A police car was heading toward them at top speed. They were traveling Highway 16 and the black-topped road stretched ahead.

Mickey bit his lip. He had to make a decision quickly. There were only a few moments before the police car would catch up to their station wagon. Mickey could tell J.E. to step hard on the gas pedal to try to outrun the police or to obey the law and pull over.

Mickey believed in obeying the law. If he were back home in New York City, he'd have chosen to pull over in a heartbeat. But here in Mississippi in 1964, the laws weren't always upheld fairly. Even worse, local police often made up their own rules. He glanced once more at the approaching police car and wondered, "What should you do if you don't trust the police?"

The problem was that the Neshoba County officers were not coming to protect Mickey. They were coming to get him. His name was on a "hit list," a list of people who some men in town wanted dead. Mickey suspected that the local sheriff was working with these men and would help them track down people on the list.

He sighed. He realized that Andrew and J.E. were also in danger, simply because they were in his company.

Looking over at the speedometer, Mickey checked to make sure that J.E. wasn't speeding. He definitely wasn't swerving or driving badly. None of them had stolen anything or broken any other laws. There was only one possible reason they were being followed. It was just as J.E. had said. The officers were "bringing nothing but trouble."

Chapter Two

Where liberty is, there is my country.

—Benjamin Franklin

 **Michael (Mickey) Schwerner** and his wife, Rita, had moved from New York City to Meridian, Mississippi, in January 1964. Raised in a Jewish home, he was not outwardly religious, but his Jewish roots gave him a deep appreciation of a world based on justice, righteousness, and equality for all people. He was inspired by Jewish leaders throughout history who had witnessed oppression and had tried to stop it.

He'd come to Mississippi in the footsteps of those who came before him: the biblical prophets, the rabbis, and all who fought for social justice. Mickey was determined to be part of that chain. With his own hands, he would make the world a better place to live.

In 1964, the South was still segregated. Blacks and whites lived their lives separately. Even though slavery had long been abolished, black people did not yet have the same rights and freedoms that their white neighbors enjoyed.

Up north, where Mickey had come from, things were far from perfect, but they were definitely better. Blacks and whites attended the same schools, ate at the same restaurants, and used the same public restrooms.

Mickey believed in integration and that all people should be treated equally. During his college days at Cornell University in upstate New York, when a black student hadn't been allowed to join his fraternity, Mickey lobbied to have that rule overturned.

At the age of twenty-four, he had come to Mississippi to fight against segregation.

Chapter Three

It is a worthy thing to fight for one's freedom;
it is another sight finer
to fight for another man's.

—Mark Twain

Mickey and his wife, Rita, had come to Mississippi as part of Freedom Summer, a program established by a group of civil rights organizations. Their goals were to register voters, and to improve education for black children attending separate, but unequal, public schools.

Volunteers would establish thirty Freedom Schools throughout the state to teach black history, as well as reading and math, and would register people to vote.

Even though the Fifteenth Amendment to the Constitution, adopted in 1870, had given people of all races the right to vote, only six percent of Mississippi blacks were registered. Some didn't know how to register. Many were afraid. Local officials kept blacks from voting through fear and intimidation, which included beatings. Freedom Summer was going to change that.

The Ku Klux Klan (KKK), a group of white segregationists, had organized to stop the Freedom Summer volunteers. KKK members liked living in a segregated society and would stop at nothing to keep it that way. The dangerous men who wanted Mickey and other civil rights workers out of Mississippi were members of the KKK.

There were officers in the Neshoba police department who were also members of the KKK. Mickey was pretty certain that it was one of these officers honking his squad car horn and demanding that J.E. pull over. But there was no way to be certain.

"Pull your car to the side of the road," a man shouted through a bullhorn.

Mickey glanced in his sideview mirror again. The police car was right behind them now. He listened to the blaring siren, still unsure what to do.

"Should I put the pedal to the metal?" J.E. asked Mickey.

"What can they do to us?" Andrew asked. "We haven't done anything wrong."

"They could kill us," J.E. replied, fear in his voice.

"Or maybe they will just ask us some questions and then let us go," Andrew countered.

Both men turned to Mickey. He was their team leader. It was up to him to make the decision. He took a hard look at each of his traveling companions. They were good men, and he desperately wanted to protect them.

Chapter Four

It isn't enough to talk about peace,
One must believe in it.
And it isn't enough to believe in it.
One must work for it.
—Eleanor Roosevelt

Andrew Goodman had been in Mississippi for only one day. His optimism about the future was contagious, and it was reflected in the way he looked at the world. Just minutes before, as they passed a lush hill covered with flowers, he had commented, "Mississippi sure is a beautiful part of the country." But now, he was learning about its dangerous brand of "law enforcement."

Like Mickey, Andrew was Jewish and was inspired by Judaism's teachings. He had come to Mississippi to lend his voice to the cause of social justice. Before he'd become involved in civil rights work, Andy had been an actor and had even performed off-Broadway. He loved acting but was more interested in people. So he changed his college major to anthropology and signed up to volunteer for Freedom Summer.

Mickey had met Andrew in Oxford, Ohio, at a training session for new volunteers. From the moment they met, he was certain that Andrew would make a valuable contribution.

Chapter Five

Let us have faith that right makes might, and in that faith let us to the end dare to do our duty as we understand it.

—Abraham Lincoln

James Earl Chaney (J.E.) would also make his name in history. Mickey could feel it in his bones. The two had met when Mickey first arrived in the South and had become fast friends.

J.E. was born twenty-one years earlier in Meridian, Mississippi, in Lauderdale County, which borders Neshoba County. His future as a civil rights activist began at the age of sixteen, when he was suspended from school for wearing a button that supported the NAACP (National Association for the Advancement of Colored People).

Later, he attended Harris Junior College
but left to work with his father, a plasterer.
He spent his free time volunteering in the
Meridian office of CORE, the Congress of Racial
Equality, where Mickey had just been hired as
office director.

As a black person, J.E. could more easily
earn the confidence of community leaders who
didn't trust white people. It wasn't long before
Mickey urged him to become a full-time paid
staff member.

Mickey smiled to himself as he remembered Chaney's silly side. Outwardly, J.E. seemed shy and quiet, serious and determined. But when they were alone, he could make Mickey laugh like no one else could.

Mickey took one last look at J.E. before turning his eyes back to the road. J.E. was not being funny right this minute. He wasn't being shy either. By his words and by the expression on his face, J.E. made it perfectly clear that he thought they were in terrible danger.

Chapter Six

We stand for FREEDOM.

— John F. Kennedy

For six months, Mickey and J.E. had been traveling together throughout small towns in Mississippi. At each stop, they met with the leaders of local black churches, asking if they would be willing to have their buildings used to host Freedom Schools. CORE would provide the teachers. They simply needed locations.

The pastor at Mount Zion Methodist Church in Longdale had agreed, and Mickey and J.E. had hurried to Ohio to gather teachers for the new school. There they met Andrew. When they heard that the KKK had burned down the Longdale church to prevent the Freedom School from opening, they rushed back to Mississippi to assess the damage.

Only a few hours ago, they'd arrived in town and driven to Mount Zion. They found the church in ruins. Fire had ripped through the building, tearing down the roof and leaving nothing but ash.

As they drove back to the CORE office in Meridian, Mickey was more determined than ever to open the schools. But even though they had a list of potential sites and pastors to contact, he wondered if anyone would be brave enough to offer their buildings after what had happened at Mount Zion.

The flashing lights and blaring siren of the police car brought Mickey's attention back to the decision he had to make. Finding a new school site would have to wait. First, he needed to deal with the police.

He considered telling J.E. to go ahead, stomp on the gas pedal, and speed up. Maybe they could outrun the police. Then he changed his mind. Perhaps it was better to see what the officer wanted. He went back and forth a few times, shaking his head over his options.

Finally, Mickey made his decision.

He had not come to Mississippi to break the law, even though there were a lot of bad laws that needed changing. He was better than the men who turned their backs on what was legal and right. He was stronger and more determined. The world was changing. Crooked police, backward-thinking men, or even the masked and hooded members of the KKK couldn't stop progress.

Someday blacks and whites would be equal. They would go to the same schools, live in the same communities, and share jobs and friends. Their children would play together in peace.

There would be blacks in senior positions
in government, and someday, a black person
would be elected president of the United States.

Mickey, Andrew, and J.E. were in Mississippi
to lend their voices to the cause of justice,
righteousness, and freedom. Unlawful men might
be able to stop their car, but not their mission.

On the afternoon of June 21, 1964, Mickey Schwerner took a long last look at his friends and colleagues and made his decision.

J.E. slowed the blue Ford station wagon to a crawl and pulled over to the side of the road. The police car pulled up beside them.

The three men sat in silence, waiting to see what would happen next.

MISSING
CALL FBI

THE FBI IS SEEKING INFORMATION CONCERNING THE DISAPPEARANCE AT PHILADELPHIA, MISSISSIPPI, OF THESE THREE INDIVIDUALS ON JUNE 21, 1964. EXTENSIVE INVESTIGATION IS BEING CONDUCTED TO LOCATE GOODMAN, CHANEY, AND SCHWERNER, WHO ARE DESCRIBED AS FOLLOWS:

ANDREW GOODMAN	JAMES EARL CHANEY	MICHAEL HENRY SCHWERNER

RACE:	White	Negro	White
SEX:	Male	Male	Male
DOB:	November 23, 1943	May 30, 1943	November 6, 1939
POB:	New York City	Meridian, Mississippi	New York City
AGE:	20 years	21 years	24 years
HEIGHT:	5'10"	5'7"	5'9" to 5'10"
WEIGHT:	150 pounds	135 to 140 pounds	170 to 180 pounds
HAIR:	Dark brown; wavy	Black	Brown
EYES:	Brown	Brown	Light blue
TEETH:		Good: none missing	
SCARS AND MARKS:		1 inch cut scar 2 inches above left ear.	Pock mark center of forehead, slight scar on bridge of nose, appendectomy scar, broken leg scar.

SHOULD YOU HAVE OR IN THE FUTURE RECEIVE ANY INFORMATION CONCERNING THE WHEREABOUTS OF THESE INDIVIDUALS, YOU ARE REQUESTED TO NOTIFY ME OR THE NEAREST OFFICE OF THE FBI. TELEPHONE NUMBER IS LISTED BELOW.

On June 21, 1964, Michael Schwerner, James Earl Chaney, and Andrew Goodman were stopped by Deputy Sheriff Cecil Price for an alleged traffic violation. They were taken to a jail in Neshoba County.

After being held for seven hours, they paid a $25 fine and were allowed to leave. It was already dark outside when they got into their car to head back to the CORE office in Meridian.

On their way out of town, two cars carrying Ku Klux Klan members, tipped off by the local police, ambushed their station wagon. For weeks, local law enforcement officers, aided by the FBI, searched for the missing men. Their bodies were found buried in an earthen dam, forty-four days after they disappeared. They had been brutally beaten and shot.

On June 21, 2005, Edgar Ray Killen, an outspoken KKK member, was found guilty of murdering the three men. It had taken forty-one years, but justice had finally been served.

The memory of Schwerner, Chaney, and Goodman has sustained Civil Rights activists for generations, and inspired songs and poems. The good work of these three men resulted in the establishment of more than thirty Freedom Schools throughout Mississippi.

The inscription on James Chaney's grave sums up their lives:

There are those who are alive
Yet will never live,
There are those who are dead
Yet will live forever,
Great deeds inspire and encourage the living.